D1445269

This 1993 edition published by Derrydale Books,
distributed by Outlet Book Company, Inc.,
a Random House Company, 40 Engelhard Avenue,
Avenel, New Jersey 07001

Random House
New York · Toronto · London · Sydney · Auckland

© Peter Haddock Limited, Bridlington, U.K.
Printed in Singapore

ISBN 0-517-08664-6

Little Red Riding Hood

Retold & Illustrated by John Patience

DERRYDALE BOOKS
New York · Avenel, New Jersey

One day Red Riding Hood's mother baked a pie. "Put on your cloak and hood and go and see how Granny is," she said. "I fear she is not very well. Take this pie and give her a kiss. Make sure you go the long way round and don't take the short cut through the wood!"

So Red Riding Hood set off for her grandmother's house. But when she came to the wood she forgot her mother's warning and took the short cut. She had not gone far when she met a woodcutter. "Take care," he said gravely. "The wood is a very dangerous place for a little girl. Keep to the path and hurry on your way."

Well, Red Riding Hood took no notice of what the woodcutter had told her. She dilly dallied along the way and stopped to pick a bunch of wild flowers for her granny.

Alas, a big bad wolf was prowling around looking for his lunch and spied Red Riding Hood amongst the flowers. He had a mind to eat her up there and then but he could hear the sound of the woodcutter's axe and knew he must be working close by, so the wolf dared not show himself.

The wolf ran on ahead and waited for Red Riding Hood further along the path. "Good morning," he said politely, walking alongside the little girl. "Where are you going this fine morning?" "I'm going to see my granny," said Red Riding Hood. "She's not very well and I'm taking her a pie and these flowers." "And where does your old granny live?" asked the wolf. "At the far side of the wood," replied Red Riding Hood. "Well, I mustn't keep you," said the wolf. "Goodbye now." He watched Red Riding Hood out of sight then bounded off into the woods.

The wolf took the shortest way through the woods to Granny's cottage. He was already thinking about his next meal as he knocked on the door! "Who's there?" called Granny. "It's Little Red Riding Hood," replied the wolf, making his usually gruff voice sound very small and squeaky. "I've brought you a pie and some flowers, Grandma." Granny was in bed and not very well, so she cried, "Pull up the latch and come in."

The wolf pulled up the latch, went in, leapt upon the old lady and gobbled her up. Then he put on Granny's cap and spectacles and jumped into bed to wait for Red Riding Hood.

After a while, Little Red Riding Hood arrived and knocked on the cottage door. "Who's there?" asked the wolf, doing his best to make his voice sound like Granny's. "It's Little Red Riding Hood with a pie from Mother," came the reply. "Come in, dear," called the wolf. Red Riding Hood thought her granny sounded rather strange, but she opened the door and stepped inside. She saw a figure in bed, wearing a nightcap and spectacles, with the sheets pulled up to the chin.

"Grandmamma, how strange you look today!" said Red Riding Hood. "What big eyes you have." "All the better to see you with, my dear," replied the wolf. "What big ears you have!" "All the better to hear you with, my dear," replied the wolf. "And, oh Grandmamma!" cried the little girl, "what great big teeth you have!" "All the better to eat you with!" growled the wolf. And, saying this, he leapt out of bed to grab Red Riding Hood! "Help!" screamed Red Riding Hood. "Help! Save me!"

At that moment the door was thrown open and in rushed the woodcutter. He had been passing by on his way home and had heard Red Riding Hood's scream. Whoosh! He swung his great axe and chopped off the wicked wolf's head. And, good gracious me! Would you believe it – out popped Granny! The old lady was a little shaken by her adventure, but otherwise quite well, with not a scratch on her!

"Do you know?" said Granny. "What I could do with now is a nice cup of tea." So they all had tea and ate the delicious pie which Red Riding Hood's mother had baked.

Later, as it was growing dark, the woodcutter lifted Red Riding Hood on to his shoulders and carried her home through the woods. You can imagine how surprised her mother was to hear the story!